AMM

*Is Ahead of Her Time*

Read more about Aleca's
adventures in book 1:

*Aleca Zamm Is a Wonder*

# ALECA*ZAMM
## Is Ahead of Her Time

## GINGER RUE

Aladdin

NEW YORK LONDON TORONTO SYDNEY NEW DELHI

**ALADDIN**

An imprint of Simon & Schuster Children's Publishing Division
1230 Avenue of the Americas, New York, New York 10020
First Aladdin paperback edition June 2017
Text copyright © 2017 by Ginger Stewart
Cover illustrations copyright © 2017 by Zoe Persico
Also available in an Aladdin hardcover edition.
All rights reserved, including the right of reproduction in whole or in part in any form.
ALADDIN and related logo are registered trademarks of Simon & Schuster, Inc.
For information about special discounts for bulk purchases, please contact
Simon & Schuster Special Sales at 1-866-506-1949 or business@simonandschuster.com.
The Simon & Schuster Speakers Bureau can bring authors to your live event. For more
information or to book an event, contact the Simon & Schuster Speakers Bureau
at 1-866-248-3049 or visit our website at www.simonspeakers.com.
Cover designed by Karin Paprocki
Interior designed by Hilary Zarycky
The text of this book was set in ITC New Baskerville.
Manufactured in the United States of America 0517 OFF
2 4 6 8 10 9 7 5 3 1
Library of Congress Control Number 2016952126
ISBN 978-1-4814-7064-3 (hc)
ISBN 978-1-4814-7063-6 (pbk)
ISBN 978-1-4814-7065-0 (eBook)

In memory of Mandy Latner (1974–2016),
who loved children and books

# CONTENTS

# ALECA*ZAMM
## Is Ahead of Her Time

# ✳ 1 ✳

## What's Worse Than Getting in Trouble? Waiting to Get in Trouble!

"Where's Aunt Zephyr?" I asked my mom as soon as I hopped into the car after school.

"And hello to you, too," said my mom.

"Sorry," I said. "Hi, Mom. Where's Aunt Zephyr? Is she waiting for us at home?"

"I'm afraid not," my mother replied.

"Well, where is she?" I asked. "Will she be back soon?"

"I don't know," answered my mom. "I haven't seen her all day."

This was not good news. Because ever since lunch that day, all I'd been able to think about was talking to my weird, Wonder-ful aunt Zephyr. I hadn't been able to focus on anything else—not my schoolwork; not my best friend, Maria; not even my awesome birthday skating party happening the next day.

The reason I was thinking about Aunt Zephyr was because she was the only other person I knew who was a Wonder, like me. At least, that was what Aunt Zephyr called us— Wonders. The word referred to people who were able to do amazing, unusual things. Aunt Zephyr could think herself anywhere in the world she wanted to go. I could stop time—which, by the way, was something I was not supposed to do. Ever again.

But I had. That very day, in the school lunchroom.

I mean, I'd had a good reason and everything. At least I'd thought so.

Trouble was, I had kind of gotten caught.

Maybe.

Possibly?

Probably.

And so I needed to run this information by Aunt Zephyr immediately.

"I wish I knew when she was coming back," I said.

"Unfortunately, your aunt left without a word to anyone. I find that to be an *egregious* lack of good manners." I didn't know what that word meant, but Mom had dragged it out and emphasized it—"ee-GREEEE-gee-us"—so I figured it must mean something really bad if she took that long to say it. Then Mom added, "But what do I know? I'm just a Dud, after all."

My mom is usually very good-natured. In fact, her first name is Harmony, which is perfect because she has a talent for getting along with almost everybody all the time. But she seemed pretty annoyed about Aunt Zephyr's leaving without telling her. Plus, she hadn't been too thrilled when Aunt Zephyr had called her a Dud, which I guess might sound kind of harsh if you happen to be a Dud, but Aunt Zephyr doesn't mean it to be hurtful. That is just what she calls regular people who aren't Wonders like us. My sister and both of my parents are Duds, and so is everyone else I know except for Aunt Zephyr.

Oh, and apparently at least one other person.

I knew this because Duds are stopped along with everything else when I stop time, so they don't even know it's happening. I thought everyone at my school was a Dud, since everybody stops when I stop time. Well, I *thought* everybody stopped. But earlier today when I stopped time in the lunchroom, I saw someone's head move outside the window. It caught my eye, seeing as how it was the only motion there was. When time stops, trees stop blowing in the wind because the wind stops blowing. Stuff that was thrown up into the air stays there instead of falling back down. Birds and bugs stop flying and just float. A splash of water stands up stiff and stays there. Everything looks just like in a photograph. Nothing moves. Nothing makes a sound.

Except for other Wonders.

So when I saw the movement outside the lunchroom window, I ran to see who it was. But I didn't find anyone. All I could tell from the brief glimpse I'd had was that the person's hair hadn't been orange-sherbet-colored, so I knew it wasn't Aunt Zephyr.

Either another Wonder lived in our town, or someone had come looking for me. Aunt Zephyr had warned me that some Duds might be aware of us. That was one reason why I wasn't supposed to stop time, because there could be dangerous Duds lurking. Who knew?

So the person outside the lunchroom could've been a Dud who had figured out a way to become immune to Wonder-ing, or it could have been another Wonder who was not Aunt Zephyr. I had no idea how many other Wonders existed in the world, but it seemed unlikely that there would be another one in our little town of Prophet's Porch, Texas. I had to find out who it was and what they wanted.

But since Aunt Zephyr could think herself places in the blink of an eye, right then she could have been anywhere in the world.

I had to find Aunt Zephyr, fast, and ask her what to do about the person I'd seen outside the lunchroom window.

But how?

# ❋ 2 ❋

## Sticky Situations
## and Sneeze Stifling

When I got home, I looked all over the house. "Aunt Zephyr?" I called. I thought maybe she might be back from wherever she'd gone, but she didn't answer.

It was lucky for me that Dylan wasn't home from choir practice yet. She might have asked questions about why I was so worried about finding Aunt Zephyr. I didn't think Dylan was particularly fond of our aunt.

"Aleca, is something wrong?" my mom asked. "Did something else . . . happen?"

My mom and dad knew all about my being a Wonder. My mom had been pretty freaked out when she'd heard, because until then she hadn't known that Wonders even existed, and she'd certainly never met one. My dad hadn't been too surprised because he'd known that his dad and his uncle Zander and his aunt Zephyr were Wonders. Dad was a Dud because probably Wonderness skipped a generation or something. But at least he'd known what Wonders were. I guess that was why he hadn't had to take a headache pill and go lie down when he'd heard the news, the way Mom had.

"Aleca," Mom said now. "Is there something you're not telling me?"

9

I mumbled, "I kinda stopped time again today."

"You what?"

"I kinda stopped time again."

"Kinda?" my mom said. "Aleca, how does one 'kind of' stop time?"

She had a point.

"Okay, I stopped time," I admitted. "No 'kinda.'"

"Darling!" my mom said. She looked worried. "You know you're not supposed to do that anymore! It's dangerous!"

I felt bad, because my mom is awesome. Ever since I started kindergarten, she has put funny notes in my lunch box every day. She cuts my sandwiches into four triangles, just the way I like it. She doesn't get mad when I get a bad grade on a math test, as long as I try my hardest. She was letting me have my birthday party at the skating rink, with a cake from the fancy bakery downtown, and was even getting several of those shiny balloons that are four or five bucks a pop. (Not that you would pop them, but that is what people say—"a pop." Even about balloons.)

"I'm sorry, Mom," I said. "I was trying to help someone." I explained to her about how a lunchroom worker was about to drop a tray filled with steaming water. "I kept her from getting hurt. And I kept perfectly good hot dogs from going to waste. Two good things!"

Mom hugged me. "I understand, sweetie," she said. "But we don't know what bad things might happen if you continue using your . . . power."

"I know," I replied. I didn't have the heart

to tell her about the moving head I had seen outside the lunchroom window.

Just then the door opened. Mom and I both jumped to see who it was. But it was only Dylan.

"Choir practice got canceled." Dylan sighed. "Kelly's mom dropped me off. What's wrong with you two?"

"Wrong?" my mom asked. "Why would anything be wrong?"

"Because you both look like you just stuck your finger into an electrical socket." She meant that we looked jittery and crazy-eyed. And that is how you look after you stick your finger into an electrical socket. I know from experience. When I was little, I had trouble sometimes "making good choices" like they told us to do in preschool.

"Ha-ha-ha," my mom said. She didn't actually laugh; she said "ha-ha-ha." "Everything is fine. But you haven't seen your aunt Zephyr, have you? We've looked all over for her and don't know where she is."

"I haven't seen her," said Dylan. "You think she finally decided to leave?"

"She just got here yesterday," my mom answered.

"Long enough for me." Dylan scowled.

Mom didn't say anything.

"I've got homework," Dylan said, and went upstairs to her room.

It was only a few seconds later that we heard her scream.

Mom and I ran up the stairs to her room.

"What on earth?" Mom yelled. Aunt Zephyr was sitting on Dylan's bed, wearing

13

only a towel around her body and a towel around her hair.

"I thought you said she wasn't here!" Dylan shouted. "Scared me to death, someone sitting on my bed when I opened the door! What's she even doing in my room?"

"A thousand pardons for invading your sanctuary," said Aunt Zephyr. "My aim isn't what it used to be."

"Aim?" asked Dylan. Then she whispered to Mom, "She is such a freak!"

"Dylan," Mom said. "You haven't had a snack since you got home from school. Why don't you run down to the kitchen and pour yourself a nice glass of milk? I made chocolate chip cookies."

"Cookies?" Dylan questioned, her eyebrows arched like rainbows. "All right. But can you please get her out of here?"

"Watch yourself, Dylan," Mom cautioned. "You will treat your aunt Zephyr with respect."

Dylan rolled her eyes but was too scared of Mom to say anything back. She knew she was one smart-mouthed comment away from losing her cell phone for a week, and as a middle schooler, Dylan did not think it was physically possible to live without her phone. She stomped downstairs.

Once Dylan was gone, Mom whispered, "Zephyr, we've been worried sick! Where have you been?"

"Finland," Aunt Zephyr replied.

"Why are you wearing towels?" I asked.

"I ran into an old friend," she said. "She invited me to take a sauna with her."

"What's a sauna, and where did you take it to?" I asked.

"A sauna, my dear, is a sweat bath."

"Gross!" I said. "I wouldn't take a bath in somebody's sweat for a million bucks!"

"The sweat is one's own," Aunt Zephyr explained. "It is produced by sitting in a hot room and relaxing."

"Wait. You mean you went all the way to Finland to sit around and get sweaty—on purpose—with a friend of yours?" I asked.

"Of course. In Finland it's very rude to refuse an invitation to sauna. What choice did I have? Besides, a nice, deep sweat is so invigorating. Do I look invigorated?"

"You look kind of sticky," I stated.

"If by 'sticky' you mean 'relaxed,' then you are correct," said Aunt Zephyr.

"You might have told me you were going to Finland," said my mom.

"I assure you, Harmony, it was a spur-of-the-moment decision. Spontaneity keeps life interesting."

"Well, if you're going to be spontaneous again anytime soon, could you at least leave a note?" My mom sighed. "Aleca has something to tell you."

"What is it, little miss?" asked Aunt Zephyr.

I gulped hard, like I was trying to swallow the news so it wouldn't come out. "I stopped time again today," I blurted.

Aunt Zephyr didn't look shocked. "Of course. I already knew that," she asserted. "Just as I was telling the most marvelous story, I noticed that Vilhelmiina failed to

laugh at the best part, about the hippopota-
mus and the man in the trench coat. At first
I thought Vilhelmiina had lost her sense of
humor entirely. But then I realized that no
one could *not* laugh at the hippopotamus-
and-the-man-in-the-trench-coat story. So it
stood to reason that either Vilhelmiina was
dead or you'd stopped time again. I stepped
out of the sauna and realized no one was
moving, so I assumed the latter. But more to
the point—did we or did we not discuss this
just yesterday?" she asked flatly.

"We did," I said. "But see, I had this
idea—"

"You had an idea," Aunt Zephyr interrupted. "So did the people who created
cigarettes . . . or shoes for cats. Not all
ideas are good ones."

I repeated the story about the lunch lady and how I'd wanted to help her. Then I tried to explain my theory that if I did a good thing when I stopped time, maybe it would cancel out any bad things I had done by stopping time before. When I said it out loud, my theory sounded pretty ridiculous.

"Wait . . . don't tell me," Aunt Zephyr said. "It didn't work out as you'd hoped."

"Not exactly," I said. Then I told her and Mom about the person moving outside the lunchroom window.

"Oh, Aleca!" Mom cried. "Who?"

"That's just it," I replied. "I don't know. I went outside to look, but the person was long gone."

Aunt Zephyr didn't say anything for a while. Her eyebrows were squished together so that the skin between them made a deep eleven.

"Aren't you going to say anything?" I asked.

"I don't exactly know what to say," declared Aunt Zephyr. "This is most troubling."

"Who do you think it could be?" asked my mom.

"I have no clue," she said.

Suddenly I felt excited. "I've got an idea!" I exclaimed.

"Oh, good," Aunt Zephyr muttered. "Another idea."

"How about if you come to school with me on Monday, like maybe to read to my class or something, and while you're there, I can stop time again. Then the two of us can search for the person who was outside the lunchroom window. It will be easy to tell who it is, because the three of us will be the only ones not frozen!"

"Absolutely not!" insisted Aunt Zephyr. "We don't know whom we're dealing with. It could be someone dangerous. We can't risk you exposing yourself again. So no more time stopping. Do you understand?"

"Yes, ma'am," I said.

"I mean it, Aleca," said Aunt Zephyr. "You're causing us all a lot of needless worry."

"Speaking of needless worry, Aunt Zephyr," my mom said. "About your . . . travels? You're the only one who can help Aleca with being a Wonder. We desperately need you here. And if you must unexpectedly dash off to Finland or wherever, could you please let us know where we can contact you? If there's an emergency—"

"I assure you, Harmony," Aunt Zephyr said, "that from now on I will try to be more considerate about my spur-of-the-moment jaunts."

"Thank you," my mom replied. "I would greatly appreciate it." Mom didn't look relieved, though. She still looked really tense, and she rubbed her forehead like she had a whopper of a headache. "I'm going to check on Dylan," she said.

"Your mother is upset," Aunt Zephyr fretted after Mom left the room. "That is regrettable."

"You got off easy," I asserted.

"I would never worry your mother on purpose," Aunt Zephyr said. "You see, Aleca, between you, me, and the fence post, I didn't exactly intend to go to Finland today."

I looked around but didn't see any fence posts. Also, I didn't understand what Aunt Zephyr meant about not going to Finland on purpose. "You went to Finland by accident?"

"Yes." She groaned.

"Oh," I said. "Well, why didn't you just tell Mom that? Then she wouldn't be upset with you."

"I'd rather her be upset with me and think I'm inconsiderate than have her worry herself sick," Aunt Zephyr said. "If she knew the truth, she'd be a nervous wreck."

"What is the truth?"

Aunt Zephyr hesitated. "The truth is, I can't always help it when I teleport some-where."

"You can't?"

"No," she replied. "As I age, my Wonder ability seems to be going the way of the rest of my abilities. Like my joints, my teleportation is getting a little . . . creaky and unpredictable."

I guess I scrunched up my face, because Aunt Zephyr tried to explain.

"When you get older, things you took for granted all your life stop working the way they used to. Like sometimes if I bend over to lace my shoe, I pull a muscle in my back. Or I bruise easily because my skin has become thinner. Or I have trouble seeing the words in a book."

"Is that because of those big flaps of skin? Do they fall over your eyeballs and make you not able to see?" After I said it, I felt kind of bad, like maybe that was one of those thoughts I should've kept to myself.

Aunt Zephyr cleared her throat. "No, that wasn't what I meant, but thank you for noticing." Then she immediately went to Dylan's mirror and pulled the skin flaps away from her eyeballs. "What I meant was that my eyesight is getting worse. And my back is more temperamental. And, as you so kindly pointed out, my skin is not only thin but also flappy. I'm old, Aleca. And everything is starting to go. Including my teleportation."

"But your Wonder ability isn't part of your body," I said. "It doesn't sag or creak like your body parts."

"It's part of my brain, though. The brain is like a muscle, Aleca," she said. "It gets old and out of shape too. I find that I can't remember things the way I used to. I walk into a room sometimes and forget why I went in there. Or I tell someone something I've already told them, but I don't remember telling them the first time. The teleportation difficulties are the same. As a child I had limited control over my teleporting, but I practiced until I gained mastery over it. I was able to decide whether I wanted to think myself somewhere or not. As a young woman I could go wherever I wanted, whenever I wanted. I could think of a place but control whether or not I went there. But lately . . . I don't know. Oh, how can I explain it? Aleca, have you ever tried to stifle a sneeze?"

"Yes," I said. "Because my sneezes are real doozies—very loud and embarrassing."

Aunt Zephyr smiled. "And can you ⸱
yourself from sneezing if you try?"

"Most of the time," I replied. "But not
always."

"Then you have some idea of what I'm
trying to tell you," she said. "My teleportation is kind of like a sneeze. And the older I
get, the less I'm able to stifle it."

# ❊ 3 ❊

# Roller-Skating
# and Nose Rubbing

Worrying about stifling her teleportation did not cause Aunt Zephyr to lose any sleep that night. She gorilla snored, just like she had the night she'd arrived.

Maybe she wasn't losing any sleep, but I was. I don't think it was because of the snoring, though. I think it was the worrying.

Aunt Zephyr had come to help me learn how to be a Wonder, but it seemed like she wasn't able to even help herself sometimes.

28

And I wasn't supposed to tell my parents about her not being able to control her teleportation, on account of Aunt Zephyr didn't want to worry them. Well, neither did I, but I also sort of wished somebody could worry about it besides just me. Worrying is supposed to be for grown-ups, isn't it?

I think that's true, because when you're ten years old, you can worry about something only for so long before something shiny and glittery grabs your attention.

The shiny and glittery thing for me was . . . my skating party! The next day was Saturday, which meant that my tenth birthday party was finally here!

I could hardly wait to skate with my friends. Even the Hokey Pokey, which is otherwise strictly for babies, is fun when you're on wheels and there are colored lights. Also, there are races, and the winners get a free soda or slice of pizza from the concessions stand, plus, of course, the glory of beating everyone else on skates.

The only bad part about my party was that Mom didn't want anyone to get hurt feelings, so I'd had to invite my whole entire class. And probably even the ones who didn't like me would have to come anyway since their moms would not want to hurt my feelings.

Most of elementary school revolves around avoiding hurt feelings. Like when you are forced to give valentines to everyone in your class, and you spend all that time picking out the cards in the box that don't say something mushy or tell certain people how great they are, because they aren't great and you certainly don't feel any mush for them.

I had tried to argue with my mom that it hurt *my* feelings to have to invite the meanies and the crybabies and the troublemakers to my party, but apparently *my* feelings didn't matter. Sometimes my mom misunderstands the whole hurt-feelings thing. I think Birthday Girl status should beat hurt feelings of classmates, kind of the way rock beats scissors and paper beats rock.

I almost didn't even care if Madison and Jordan showed up and treated me like dirt; I would ignore them anyway. Plus, Maria was definitely coming, and what is better than a skating party with your best friend? (The answer is . . . not much.)

Maria was coming over early Saturday

afternoon; we were going to the party together and then she would spend the night. Mom and Dad weren't sure the sleepover was the best idea anymore, given all that had happened in the last few days with my Wonder ability and Aunt Zephyr showing up, but since we had made the plans a few weeks before, they said we should just go with it.

When Maria got to my house, she made a face and asked, "What is that awful noise?"

"Aunt Zephyr is taking a nap," my mother replied.

"She snores," I explained. "A lot."

"M-o-o-o-om!" Dylan whined. The way she dragged it out made it sound like "Mom" had a whole string of *o*'s in it.

"It won't kill you for one night," Mom said.

"Easy for you to say." Dylan groaned. "She's not sleeping in *your* room."

Maria and I watched TV for a little while and ate snacks, and then, before we knew it, it was time to get ready to go to the rink. Aunt Zephyr's snoring had stopped, which made me glad in a way but also reminded me to worry. What if the snoring was gone because Aunt Zephyr was gone, and gone without meaning to be gone?

"I need to check on something," I told Maria. "Be right back."

Dylan was downstairs on the computer, so I slipped into her room without asking permission. I am not supposed to do that, but it's not every day that you have to check to see if your aunt has accidentally gone to Finland during her nap. The bedcovers were dented as if someone had recently been lying there, but the bed was empty. I looked around but didn't see Aunt Zephyr anywhere.

*Oh no,* I thought. *Where could she be?*

"Hi there!" chirped a loud and cheerful voice.

"Ahhh!" I called. I turned toward the closet, where Aunt Zephyr was standing. She was wearing a short, twirly purple-and-black skirt with a purple-and-black blouse and patterned black tights. She even had on matching black glasses, and her orange hair hung down around her face except where it kind of stuck out on the sides. "You scared me," I said. "I thought you'd gone missing again."

"Oh, not today," she said. "That's why I

made sure to get a good nap. It works wonders on the Wonders." She tapped the side of her head. "I feel like a million bucks. Do I look like a million bucks?"

What was I supposed to say? "Maybe eight hundred thousand?" That seemed like a big enough number to still be generous.

"What? Don't you like my outfit?"

I'm not supposed to lie, but I'm also not supposed to say mean things. Mom and Dad always tell me, *If you can't say something nice, don't say anything at all.* So that was what I did. . . . I didn't say anything at all.

"Cat got your tongue?" joked Aunt Zephyr. "I'll have you know that this was all the rage the last time I went roller-skating."

"When was that?" I asked.

"Let's see. . . . I believe it was . . . Oh yes. It was on the Embarcadero Freeway in San Francisco back in the late 1980s after an earthquake! Oh, what fun! I can hardly wait for your party!"

"You're coming to my party?" I asked. "And you're actually going to skate?"

"Of course and of course," she replied. "Why wouldn't I?"

"I don't know," I mumbled. "Aren't you kind of old for roller-skating?"

"Bah!" answered Aunt Zephyr. "You're only as old as you feel!"

This was odd, even for Aunt Zephyr, which is saying a lot, seeing as how Aunt Zephyr was pretty much always odd. Hadn't she just been telling me how she was old and falling apart? And now she was acting like a spring chicken. I wasn't sure why people said "spring chicken," but I supposed maybe the spring was when chickens got born? Either way, Aunt Zephyr was acting like she thought she was young.

"Are you sure you should be skating?" I asked.

"You only live once," she noted. "And as I recall, skating is exhilarating! You should have seen us back then! We called ourselves the Midnight Rollers. It was a double-decker freeway, completely closed after the quake. Oh, it was glorious! Such a shame they had to tear it down."

"There might have been more room on the freeway for skating than there is at the rink," I observed. "It can get kind of crowded on Saturday nights. There's not a lot of entertainment in Prophet's Porch, and sometimes the high schoolers go there for something to do. They skate really fast. I always hold Maria's hand when we start out, just because there's less chance of them mowing down two of us together."

"Nonsense!" proclaimed Aunt Zephyr. "I will not be intimidated by adolescents on wheels! I intend to skate, and I intend to enjoy myself immensely!"

"Suit yourself," I said.

Maria came upstairs, calling my name. "That's my friend Maria," I told Aunt Zephyr. "I'll introduce you. But please don't freak her out."

"How would I do that?" Aunt Zephyr questioned. I think she really didn't know.

"Oh, there you are," Maria said. "What're you doing in Dylan's room? Won't she kill you if she catches you in here?"

"I was just checking on my aunt," I replied. "Maria, meet Aunt Zephyr. Aunt Zephyr, meet Maria."

"Enchanted," Aunt Zephyr said. She leaned down and rubbed her nose against Maria's nose. Maria stepped back and looked at me, confused. And, as I'd predicted, she seemed really freaked out.

"*¿Qué diablo?*" Maria shouted. Which basically means "What the fladoodlecakes?" which was a perfectly reasonable question.

"That's how people greet each other in New Zealand," Aunt Zephyr informed us.

"Aunt Zephyr," I said through clenched teeth. "This isn't New Zealand."

"Nevertheless, it is a charming greeting, don't you think?" she asked.

"Not so much," I said.

"Bah!" said Aunt Zephyr. "You should get out more. Well, I'm going downstairs to find your mother."

When Aunt Zephyr had left the room, I told Maria, "Don't ask."

"I wouldn't know where to start," said Maria.

"Let's go get ready for the party," I suggested. "I'm going to wear my new birthday outfit! It's a green jacket with fringe at the bottom, which will swish when I skate. Also, I have leggings and a flouncy skirt!"

"Flouncy?" asked Maria. "How flouncy?"

"Extra flouncy," I replied. "I am going to

flounce all over the place in that thing!"

As Maria and I went to my room to change, I hoped the weirdest part of our night had already happened.

Nope.

# ✳ 4 ✳

## Every Party Has Its Pooper

Just as I'd predicted, the roller rink was
packed. Probably because it was raining outside so everybody wanted to do an indoor
activity. There were families with little kids,
and there were groups of teenagers. The
only place we had to ourselves was the party
room, where Mom had put the balloons,
drinks, and cake. Even though this cake
could not possibly be as tasty as the lemon-
raspberry surprise Mom had made on my

actual birthday, this one was prettier. It was white with colorful stripes down the sides and a big, bright green bow on top. The bow was made of fondant. I knew that from all those bakery battle shows on TV. I had never actually eaten fondant before, so now was my chance.

Almost everybody from my class showed up at the party—even Madison and Jordan. They probably had no choice: Madison's mom really likes my mom. I think it made her sad when Madison stopped being friends with Maria and me. When she saw my mom, she hugged her and said, "Harmony! So great to see you!"

"I'm glad Madison could make it," said my mom. "I haven't seen you in such a long time, Madison. How are you?"

43

"Fine," mumbled Madison. She rolled her eyes at Jordan, who was glued to her like always. Madison's mom cleared her throat, which meant Madison was about to be in trouble if she didn't watch her step.

"She's a little tired, that's all." Her mom laughed uncomfortably. "Thanks so much for inviting her. We hope you like your present!" I could tell by how she said it that Madison hadn't had a thing to do with picking out my present, but that was fine by me. Madison probably would have given me a stinky, dead rat if she could've gotten away with it.

Her mom continued, "And look at you, Miss Birthday Girl! Aren't you just as pretty as a picture? And getting so grown-up!"

"Thank you," I said. I wondered why Madison couldn't be sweet like her mom.

"And good to see you, Maria," Madison's mother went on. She looked at my mom with a sad smile. "I do miss the days of the Three Amigas."

"We must find the time to get the girls together for a playdate one of these days!" my mom yelled over the music. She was just saying that to be nice. There was no way that was ever going to happen, and we all knew it. Ever since Madison had become a soccer girl, she thought she was way too cool for Maria and me.

"Madison, why don't you and Jordan take Aleca's gifts in there?" Her mom motioned toward the party room.

"Great idea," acknowledged my mom. "Aleca, show them which room we're in."

Madison and Jordan hung back from

Maria and me, walking so slowly that you'd think they were older than Aunt Zephyr. They were slumped over and growly faced, like we were walking them to a dungeon. When we finally got into the party room, I said, "Here we are."

Madison declared, "We didn't pick these presents out. Our moms bought them. We don't even know what they are."

"Thank you," I responded.

"We only came because our moms made us!" snapped Jordan.

"Don't do me any favors," I urged them. "You can leave now, as far as I care."

"I wish!" whined Madison. "I can't believe I'm at such a babyish party."

"My party is not babyish," I argued. "In case you didn't notice, my cake has a fondant bow."

"Ooh, I'm so impressed," Jordan gibed. I would've liked to stop time and shove both of their faces into my beautiful, fondant-bowed birthday cake, but I knew better. No time stopping. Not even if it seemed like a really good idea.

"It's time to get our skates," Madison announced to Jordan. "You go ahead. I'll be right behind you." Then Madison said to me, "Don't worry. I've got a special present just for you, Aleca Zamm."

"Oh yeah? What's that?" I asked.

"You think you got away with what you did at school the other day, don't you? But I'm going to tell on you!"

I gulped. "What are you talking about?"

Madison grinned wickedly. "You know exactly what I'm talking about! You didn't really think you could get away with it, did you? I *know* things. And I'm going to tell everyone! I am going to make sure every-one knows who you *really* are, Aleca Zamm!" Then she laughed like a villain and followed after Jordan.

"Wow. *Feliz cumpleaños*," Maria commented. "That's a nice way to treat someone on her birthday!"

"For reals," I said.

"What do you think she meant when she said she was going to tell on you?" asked Maria.

I had a bad feeling. I was so scared, I was even shaking a little bit. Could Madison know about me stopping time?

I couldn't let Maria see that I was upset. If she did, she'd get suspicious. I needed to get out of that party room, briefly ditch Maria, and find Aunt Zephyr . . . fast.

"I don't know what Madison was talking about, and I don't even care," I explained. "I've got roller-skating, a cake with a green fondant bow, and my best friend. It's going to be a great party!"

Maria and I went to get our skates. When we sat down to lace them, I saw Aunt Zephyr get up from where she'd been sitting. She had just finished her laces. I waved her over. She rolled on the carpet to where we were. "Ha-ha!" Aunt Zephyr gloated. "Triumph!"

"Huh?" I asked.

"Triumph," answered Aunt Zephyr. "Victory. I am once again on skates, and doing just fine. And you thought I was too old!"

"You were the one who was telling me you

were old," I asserted. "Don't you remember?"

"It's true that I'm old," confessed Aunt Zephyr. "But I'm also something else, and that is spry."

"What is 'spry'?" inquired Maria.

I tried to interrupt. "Aunt Zephyr—" I began. But she talked right over me.

"'Spry,' my dear," Aunt Zephyr proclaimed, "is 'nimble and brisk.'"

Maria and I looked at each other. We didn't know "nimble" or "brisk" any more than we knew "spry."

"It's a certain zest." Aunt Zephyr smiled. I guess we still looked confused, because she added, "An energy for life. Today I choose to embrace my desire to roller-skate rather than hide behind the number that tells me I am too old for such things." She raised her hand, made a fist, and declared, "Instead of cowering from life, I choose to roll toward it on these small plastic wheels! And that, you see, is what makes me spry!"

"But you're still on the carpet, Aunt Zephyr," I stated. "The rink is a lot slicker. Also, can I talk to you for a second . . . privately?"

She ignored my request. She was too excited about skating. "Rink, shmink," she replied. "Outta my way, whippersnappers! Here I come!" She bent over and started pumping her arms as she skated toward the main floor. She reminded me of one of those bulls that charges the red capes.

"Aleca, I have a bad feeling about this," cautioned Maria. "Your aunt is old, and my *mami* says old people have fragile bones. My *abuela* broke her hip and had to be in the hospital for a long time, and she still walks funny and has to rub minty ointment on herself when it rains."

"I tried to tell Aunt Zephyr she shouldn't skate," I said. "One of those high school boys is probably going to knock her into next week. But she wouldn't listen to me."

"I sure hope she knows what she's doing," Maria fretted.

"I'm sure Aunt Zephyr can take care of herself," I insisted. "Come on! Let's go skate!" Maybe I could catch up to Aunt Zephyr and stop her long enough to tell her about Madison.

Maria and I rolled to the edge of the carpet and waited for a chance to insert ourselves into the flow of skaters. Trying to find an open spot was pretty hard. The skaters just kept coming with no break in between them, like they were waiting to run you down. Finally we found an opening. Maria gripped my hand, and we went for it. The teenagers whisked past us so fast, our hair actually blew when they went by. Once we got going, we were able to let go of each other's hands and skate as an unconnected pair.

But as the music throbbed in my ears, I could hardly focus on having any fun. How could Madison know I was a Wonder? There was just no way! Every time I'd stopped time, she'd been frozen stiff just like everybody else.

I started to worry that maybe Madison hadn't been frozen. Maybe she'd been faking! Maybe she'd been watching me the whole time, even when I'd done my nobody's-watching dances!

*No way,* I told myself. Nobody could be still that long. And no way would Madison have stayed still while I squirted glue all in her hair! A person would have to be super-committed to being sneaky to fake *that.*

Then again, I didn't know anyone else as sneaky and low-down as Madison. What if she *had* been faking, just to trick me into thinking she wasn't a Wonder?

*Think, Aleca! Think!* I told myself.

I retraced all my steps from when I'd stopped time. I thought about the times in the classroom, and then the time in the lunchroom.

*The lunchroom!*

*Madison wasn't in the lunchroom when I stopped time!*

What if that had been *her* head outside

the window? Maybe she hadn't checked out to go to the dentist at all! Maybe she'd just *said* she was going to the dentist, but really she'd been hiding out so she could lurk! If anyone would know how to lurk, I was pretty sure it was Madison.

Or what if she really had gone to the dentist and had been checking back into school, and that was when she saw me through the lunchroom window? Now that I thought about it, she had gotten back right around the time we'd returned to class after lunch.

Oh no.

Of all the rotten luck.

Madison knew my secret!

What was I going to do?

Or worse . . . what was *she* going to do?

# ✳ 5 ✳

## Aunt Zephyr Shows Off

"Aleca, this is so fun!" Maria said as we continued to skate.

If I hadn't been so worried about Madison knowing my secret, I would've agreed. The lights were pretty, pulsing in time with the music, and the deejay even started playing my favorite song. I think maybe it was also the deejay's favorite song, because he was fist-pumping to the beat, with his arms way up in the air and his head bobbing like a chicken's. One time, one of the big gold chains around his neck whacked him pretty hard in the face, but lucky for him he had on big sunglasses that absorbed most of the whack. He looked around to see if anyone had noticed, then acted like it had never happened and kept on pumping his fists.

Madison and Jordan skated past us, and Madison made a V with her fingers and held them to her eyes; then she pointed them at me and mouthed, "I'm watching you!" I felt like I'd swallowed a brick, but I couldn't let Maria see that I was upset, so I kept right on skating.

Other kids from our class skated by and would wave or say happy birthday, but of course I couldn't hear them over the music. Besides, I was on a mission. I had to find

Aunt Zephyr. It took a few minutes before I spotted her on the opposite side of the rink from us. And wow! She actually was a really good skater! She was twisting her hips to the music, spinning around, and twirling on one foot. At one point she even bent down all the way to the ground, with her hiney almost to the floor and one leg straight out! I was impressed!

The bad news was that there was no way I could catch up with her. I'd have to wait to talk to her when she wore herself out.

Soon the deejay announced it was time for the races. "All right, all right! Who's got a need for speed? Who's ready to have a blast going fast? Can I get a what-what?"

No one gave him a what-what, whatever that actually is, but that didn't stop the deejay from pretending someone had. "That's right! That's what I'm talking about!" he called, followed by a woo-hoo. He started the races with the little kids, ages four to seven.

I thought I recognized one of the boys who had lined up. "Doesn't he go to our school?" I asked Maria.

"Yeah," Maria nodded. "He's new. He's in the third grade."

"He looks too small to be in third grade," I noted.

"I think he is," remarked Maria. "He's like a genius or something. They double-double promoted him."

"What's 'double-double promoted'?"

"Well, 'double promoted' is when you skip a grade. 'Double-double promoted' is when you skip two of them at once."

"Like jumping two checkers instead of one?"

"I guess so," replied Maria. "His name is Ford Kimble. There was an article in the paper about how smart he is. He speaks a bunch of languages, and I think they said he helped invent something with some professors."

"Wow," I responded. "I wish I was that smart."

"Me too," sighed Maria. "I guess some people are just special and some of us are just regular."

I felt kind of guilty then because I knew I wasn't regular, but I also knew I couldn't tell Maria that. I felt bad keeping a secret from her, but Aunt Zephyr had made me promise not to tell anyone about being a Wonder.

The deejay was ready to start the race. "When I give the signal, remember that second place is first loser!"

He sounded the horn, and the little ones were off . . . sort of. All the little kids had some trouble on their skates because little kids just aren't that good at skating. But none of them had as much trouble as Ford Kimble. Even the four-year-olds looked like Olympic athletes compared to him. He moved his legs a few times and then quickly fell right on his bottom. He got up once, then fell back down, and then the race was over. I guess you could say he came in last place, but only if you count him as placing at all.

*"Qué lástima,"* Maria said. "I feel bad for him. Don't you feel embarrassed for him, Aleca?"

"Yeah," I agreed. "Good thing he's so smart."

But Ford didn't seem to be embarrassed. He just scooted off the rink when the race was over.

"Do you see my aunt anywhere?" I asked Maria.

"Come on!" Maria said. "Our age group is next."

Talking to Aunt Zephyr would have to wait. Again.

Maybe if I'd been able to focus, I could've won the race, but at least I beat Madison and Jordan, which was all that mattered. And maybe now I could go find Aunt Zephyr and tell her about Madison.

But before I got the chance, the dee-jay announced that it was time for the sixteen-and-older race. "Oh, come on, mamma-mias and daddi-os," said the deejay. "Get out here and show the little cats and kits how it's done! Represent, my old-school faction!"

A dad or two went out onto the rink floor, but the rest of the grown-ups shook their heads and laughed.

"No more takers?" the deejay said. "All right, then. . . ."

"I'm coming!" a woman's voice shouted from a dark corner. "Hold on!"

Three guesses who it was.

# ✳ 6 ✳

# Spry or Not, Old Bones Are Still Old Bones

Aunt Zephyr made her way onto the rink floor while most of the people cheered and clapped. My mother, though, did not clap. She walked out onto the rink (she wasn't wearing skates) and whispered something to Aunt Zephyr and tried to sort of pull her off the rink floor. But Aunt Zephyr wasn't having it. She shooed my mom away, and Mom went back to the carpeted area with a concerned look on her face.

"I think your mom is scared your aunt will hurt herself," Maria concluded.

"I think so too," I remarked. "But I'm sure she'll be fine. She did okay out there before."

"I hope you're right," Maria said.

"Maria," I said. "When your grandma broke her hip, how bad did it hurt? Like, on a scale from one to ten?"

"I think, like, an eight," Maria answered.

"Oh," I said. I hoped Aunt Zephyr knew what she was doing.

The deejay gave the signal, and they were off. A teenage boy was in the lead, but Aunt Zephyr was gaining on him. She was skating really hard and really fast. I had to hand it to her. She *was* spry.

What came next happened so fast that I couldn't be sure if it was on purpose or an accident, but the boy's right foot went in front of Aunt Zephyr's left foot, and before I knew it, the crowd of people let out a big gasp . . . because Aunt Zephyr was about to go flying through the air!

I didn't have time to think it through. All I knew was that when Aunt Zephyr fell, she would fall hard. And the other skaters would roll right over her and smoosh her. And even though she was a Wonder and was also spry, her bones were still old like Maria's grandmother's bones.

So I zoomed as fast as I could onto the rink and got almost right under Aunt Zephyr before she fell.

Then I closed my eyes, slid down so that I'd make a soft landing spot for Aunt Zephyr, and whispered, "Aleca Zamm!"

# *❄ 7 ❄*

# Applying Science to the Madison Problem

Time stopped. But Aunt Zephyr—falling on top of me suddenly and fully like a hundred-and-twenty-pound ocean wave—did not.

*Splat!*

"Ouch!" I yelled. Her right skate came down hard on my left shin, and her forehead knocked my mouth. I put my hand on my teeth to make sure they were all still there.

"What are you doing?" Aunt Zephyr barked as soon as she was able to move.

"I was saving you from breaking your hip!" I chided.

"I was most certainly *not* going to break my hip!" she complained. But then she groaned and rubbed her elbow and her side. "Well, maybe an elbow," she confessed. "Or a femur. Are you all right?"

"I guess so," I muttered. "Probably just bruised."

"One can get over a bruise," Aunt Zephyr proclaimed. "One may not get over having her ability exposed to a skating rink full of onlookers. You shouldn't have done this."

She had a point.

Wow, did she ever have a point! Where was Madison? She was probably taking a video of the whole thing. Now I'd be exposed as a Wonder and get in all sorts of trouble.

Once I was able to get Aunt Zephyr off me, I got up and looked around.

The flashing lights had stopped flashing. The popcorn in the popcorn popper hung in midpop. The people watching the race stood perfectly still with their mouths open, some with their hands covering them. My mom had her head buried in my dad's shoulder, too scared to look.

And then I spotted Madison.

She was pretending to not even be watching. If I hadn't known any better, I would've thought that Madison and Jordan were frozen on their phones, stopped in the middle of playing games.

"You really think I'm going to fall for that?" I shouted in Madison's direction. But she didn't move.

"What on earth are you going on about?" asked Aunt Zephyr. "You might as well focus on the situation here." She gestured to the boy just behind where she'd fallen. He was suspended in midair, a shocked look on his face. When I looked at him, I knew I'd done the right thing, even if it meant that Madison would tell everyone about me. Because if I hadn't stopped time, the boy would have landed right on top of Aunt Zephyr. And probably the girl behind him would have rolled right over both of them and fallen too. And then the ones behind her would have followed, just like dominoes.

"You would have been smooshed," I stated. "Look. His skates aren't even touching the ground. He was about to fall on top

70

of you. And he weighs twice what you do!"

"I suppose you're right," Aunt Zephyr acknowledged. "Foolish hubris."

"Who's Hubris?" I asked. I wondered if that was the boy's name.

"'Hubris' means 'pride,'" Aunt Zephyr answered. "It is the great downfall of heroes. They become overconfident and think they can do anything. It was pure hubris on my part to think I could out-roller-skate a bunch of teenyboppers. Learn from my mistake, Aleca. Don't let hubris get the best of you."

"Umm, yeah, speaking of hubris . . . ," I began. I told her my theory about Madison. If Madison was onto my time stopping, it was my own fault. I had hubrised that up pretty bad, thinking I could get away with it even after Aunt Zephyr had told me to stop. "So you see, it must be Madison who was outside the lunchroom window," I explained.

"Preposterous!" Aunt Zephyr declared. "She was frozen in time on the other occasions, and you saw it with your own eyes. You can't really believe that the girl would have the wherewithal to stand perfectly still while you doused her hair in glue!"

"I'm telling you, she's a sneak! I wouldn't put anything past her."

"Aleca, sometimes we can get so worried about something that we lose all sense of reason. That's what you've done. You've become irrational. But if you won't listen to reason, then I suppose we will have to solve this scientifically," Aunt Zephyr said. "Come on. I'll prove to you that Madison is not a Wonder."

We rolled over to Madison and Jordan. "Cut the act, Madison," I said. "I know you're faking."

Madison stayed motionless. I tried again. "Madison, I know you're not really frozen in time."

"That's not the scientific approach," Aunt Zephyr said. "We have to provoke an involuntary reaction."

"What does that mean?"

"It means we do something that she can't help but respond to," Aunt Zephyr explained. She snapped her fingers. "Remember yesterday when we were talking about how hard it is to stifle a sneeze? You wouldn't happen to have any black pepper on you, would you?"

I made a face.

"Of course you wouldn't," she said.

Then I got an idea. "Hey! What if I smack her really hard in the face? She couldn't help but respond to that! Especially if you let me do it as hard as I want!"

"I'm surprised at you, Aleca," Aunt Zephyr replied. "Violence is for small minds." She studied Madison for a moment, thinking. "You and she were friends once, right? Close friends?"

"Yes," I said. It made me sad to think about it, actually.

"That's it!" Aunt Zephyr said. "Where is she ticklish?"

It was so obvious, I couldn't believe I hadn't thought of it. Madison was extremely ticklish. One time when Maria and I had a sleepover at Madison's house, we tickled her, and she screamed so loud that it set off the burglar alarm!

"Her sides," I said. "Right here." I poked Madison's sides. She didn't budge.

"Are you sure you're doing it right?" asked Aunt Zephyr.

"Positive," I said. I tried a few more times with my best effort. Nothing. "Wow, Aunt Zephyr. You were right. There's no way Madison knows I'm a Wonder. She could never take this much tickling without moving."

"At least we've ruled her out," Aunt Zephyr replied. "At some point we'll still need to figure out who saw you from the lunchroom window, but for now let's get back to the matter at hand."

"Okay," I agreed. "Now what do we do?"

"Well, first I need to do this." She rolled back over to where she'd fallen, turned to the boy who'd tripped her, whacked him on the back of his head, and demanded, "Show some respect for your elders, you weasel of a whippersnapper!"

"I thought you said violence was for small minds," I said.

"That was not violence," she answered. "That was justice."

I didn't really see the difference, but it didn't seem like a good time to ask for an explanation. Aunt Zephyr turned back to the other skaters. "Now we'll have to carefully reposition these folks so that when you start time again, they won't fall over us."

"Us?" I asked.

"Yes, us," she replied. "You'll have to lie

back down on the floor underneath me. Then everyone will simply think that you rushed to catch me when I fell. When time starts again, no one will know that we moved the skaters around like balls on a billiards table. They'll just think it was a lucky accident that no one else was hurt."

"Where do we move them?" I asked.

"Let's see," mumbled Aunt Zephyr. "This will involve some precise geometric placement."

"Oh," I replied. I supposed that meant I wouldn't be much help.

"Hmmm," Aunt Zephyr started. "I must be sure to calculate the trajectory of each skater just so. I don't want to arouse suspicion by moving them too much, but I must move them enough to avert an accident."

Aunt Zephyr closed one eye and stuck out her thumb, moving her arm back and forth in front of the boy who would have fallen over her.

And that was when we heard the noise coming from the deejay booth.

# ❋ 8 ❋

# Big Wonders Come
# in Small Packages

"What was that?" I demanded.

"Who's there?" asked Aunt Zephyr, spinning around and looking wild-eyed.

"Transducers and amplifiers," a small voice mumbled.

We couldn't see anyone, but the voice was definitely coming from the deejay booth's general area. It couldn't have been the deejay, though. This was a boy's voice, and much less jazzy than the deejay's. Less jazzy and more youngish.

"Come here and show yourself!" I shouted. I yelled it like I had some kind of authority, which I didn't. Whoever this was, apparently he wasn't affected by my Wonder-ness. And if he wasn't affected by it, that meant he was probably a Wonder too. Or something else. Maybe something more powerful than a Wonder. So there was the possibility that he could wallop Aunt Zephyr and me with an ability of his own. I was pretty nervous, and I could tell that Aunt Zephyr was too. She was quiet, and Aunt Zephyr was never quiet, even when she was sleeping.

We heard some clanking around in the deejay booth and then saw the door open. Out came a boy. A small boy.

A small boy named Ford Kimble.

"Would you like to know how a sound system works?" Ford offered as he walked toward us.

I was so shocked, I could hardly speak. "How?" I pleaded.

"The equalizer unit works with the calibrated microphone and the frequency analyzer, and then from the sound booth, you have—"

"No," I interrupted. "I'm not interested in how the sound system works. I meant *how* are you having this conversation with us right now? Why aren't you frozen in time like everyone else?"

"Who are you?" Aunt Zephyr thundered.

"I'm William Ford Kimble." He bowed. Actually bowed! "You can call me Ford."

"Zephyr Grace Zamm," Aunt Zephyr declared. "You can call me Miss Zephyr." She didn't offer to shake his hand.

"You haven't answered my question," I reiterated. "Why aren't you affected by time stopping?"

"I don't know," Ford responded. "But I'd like to know. I like to know how things work. That is why I watched you in the lunchroom yesterday."

"So it was you!" I have to admit, I was relieved. Ford didn't seem like much of a threat. Something about him was a little off, but he seemed like a pretty nice kid, overall.

"Does anyone else know?" Aunt Zephyr asked.

"About Aleca in the lunchroom?" Ford

replied. "Oh no. No, no, no. I can't tell anyone about that. I wouldn't know how. I don't
know how it works yet."

"Do your parents know that you're a
Wonder?" I asked.

"A Wonder?" Ford clarified. "Is that the
same as being special? My parents say I am
special."

"Special how?" I questioned. "What can
you do?"

"I can do lots of math," Ford replied.
"And I know all the advertisements from
television and billboards by heart. And
I like to take things apart and put them
back together. That is why I don't have any
friends."

I didn't understand. I looked at Aunt
Zephyr.

"What else can you do, Ford?" Aunt Zephyr asked him gently. "I mean besides your smarts. What is your ability? You must have one, or you'd be frozen in time right now." Aunt Zephyr tried to explain to him about Wonders and Duds. Ford stared at her and then began laughing.

"When Aleca stops time," he said, "I like to hold my smooth stone." He pulled a small rock out of his pocket. "Feel it. It's very smooth." After we touched it, he held the stone so that it touched his top lip and the tip of his nose.

I looked to my aunt for an explanation. Why was this boy talking to us about rocks and numbers and sound systems? Why wouldn't he tell us what we wanted to know? "Aunt Zephyr, I thought Wonder stuff didn't happen to you until you turned ten," I remembered. "Ford's only, what, seven?"

"Seven," Ford stated. "It is a number with only two factors. That means it is prime."

"I don't know everything, Aleca," acknowledged Aunt Zephyr. "Only how it happened for those in our family. Maybe every Wonder is different. Or maybe Ford is accelerated in that, too, just like he is in school."

"Ten is the first number with two integers," Ford said. "I will add that to my notes when I get home."

"What notes do you already have?" I demanded. Maybe Ford knew more than we did. Maybe he could explain things.

"We don't have time for analysis right

now," Aunt Zephyr informed us. "Well, of course we have *time*, since time has stopped. But it's like I told you before: the more often you stop time, and the longer that time is stopped, the more likely you'll be detected. We need to fix this mess and move on. Now. Let's put the skaters where they should go."

"Physics!" Ford clapped his hands, then clapped the back of his neck. Then he pushed on the boy who was floating in the air and moved him. "This should adjust the angle of incidence enough to affect the angle of reflection just enough to avoid a collision. But not too much, because this is all a secret, isn't it?" He then positioned the other skaters just so.

"Well done," remarked Aunt Zephyr.

"Now, Ford, go back to where you were. Aleca, lie down, and I'll lie across you, just like I fell."

"Wait! I almost forgot! I'll make this quick." I did a dance—a little Irish jig kind of like what Aunt Zephyr had been doing on skates—before I went to lie down.

"And that was . . . what, exactly?" Aunt Zephyr asked.

"I was dancing like no one was watching," I said. "Because no one was. I mean, except for you and Ford. It's just this thing I promised myself I'd do whenever I stop time."

"Can we get on with it, please?" she replied.

We each took our positions. Just before I was about to start time again, Aunt Zephyr called to Ford, "We will discuss this more later. For now, zip your lips!"

"That's not possible," Ford replied.

"Don't tell anyone about this," she clarified. Ford nodded and put his rock to his lip and nose again.

"Aleca, do your thing," requested Aunt Zephyr.

"Aleca Zamm," I said.

The skaters were once again in motion, the lights pulsing, and the music booming. The boy who would have smooshed us was instead able to right himself and just missed us. Since he didn't topple, the girl behind him didn't topple either. There was no series of falling-skater dominoes like there would have been if I hadn't stopped time and we hadn't moved everyone ever so slightly. Only Aunt Zephyr and I had fallen down hard, and it wasn't actually that bad for us. The other skaters stumbled into one another but quickly righted themselves. It probably looked a lot worse than it was.

Which is probably why the deejay shouted "Ooh!" and stopped the music and turned off the strobe lights. "Everybody okay?" he asked. After we all nodded, the deejay added, "I mean, I know I'm amazing, but I didn't expect you to *fall* so hard for me!" He laughed at his own joke, but the only response he got was a few moans. "Tough crowd!" he said. Then he turned on the regular overhead lights so we could see better, and Mom rushed to Aunt Zephyr and me. Aunt Zephyr gave a thumbs-up, and everyone clapped. Once we got out of the way, the lights went back down, the music began throbbing once more, and it was like nothing had happened.

Well, as far as the Duds were concerned, at least.

For Aunt Zephyr, Ford, and me, a lot had happened.

# 9

## The Smackdown on Snitches

"Aleca, are you all right?" Maria asked as soon as Aunt Zephyr and I were back onto the carpeted area. "I barely saw you zooming out there like that! You were so brave! And good thing, too. Your aunt came down pretty hard, from what I could tell. When I saw what you were doing, I didn't think there was any way you could possibly make it in time! But you did!"

"Yeah," I affirmed. "I got a lot of good . . .

um . . . slideyness . . . from the slick floor. I got there faster than I thought I could."

Once Mom had had a chance to fuss over Aunt Zephyr and me and make sure we were both okay, Aunt Zephyr proclaimed, "Aleca, I'm in desperate need of a refreshing beverage. Let's go to your party room and procure one, shall we?"

"Oh, let me get that for you, Aunt Zephyr," insisted my mom. "Just have a seat right here and I'll bring it out to you."

"I wouldn't dream of it, Harmony, dear," said Aunt Zephyr. "Aleca and I will get it. Won't we, Aleca?"

"Come to think of it, a cold drink does sound refreshing," I remarked.

"I'm thirsty too. I'll come with you," Maria offered.

"That won't be necessary," Aunt Zephyr told her. "But thank you just the same."

I could tell that Aunt Zephyr didn't want my mom or Maria around, so I went along with it. "I'll catch you in a few minutes, Maria," I assured her. "Go ahead and enjoy skating."

Maria shrugged and went back toward the rink.

Once we were inside the empty party room, Aunt Zephyr whispered, "So, what about the boy?"

"I don't know," I responded. "What about him?"

"What does your gut tell you?" she asked. "Do we trust him? Do we not trust him?"

"He's odd, but he seems pretty harmless," I mused. "What do you think his deal is? He says weird things."

"It would seem that Ford's genius comes with a side order of social issues."

"I guess so," I agreed. "Seems like if you were that smart, making conversation would be so easy."

"As you ought to know by now, Aleca," Aunt Zephyr remarked, "things aren't always what they seem."

"That's true," I replied.

"Take me, for instance," she continued. "To the untrained eye I seem just like your average, everyday old lady."

"Oh, I wouldn't say that," I answered. I gestured to her purple-and-black getup.

"An average, everyday old lady with flair and pizzazz," she conceded. "And you seem like a perfectly normal ten-year-old girl. But we know better, don't we?"

Just then we heard a sneeze.

"Who's there?" Aunt Zephyr demanded. She skated to the door. It was already open, but we hadn't known that someone was standing next to the wall beside it, hidden from our view. "Don't you know it's impolite to eavesdrop, young lady?"

"I wasn't eavesdropping." It was Madison. For once she was without Jordan. That was unusual. But I supposed that even Jordan had to go to the bathroom on her own sometimes. "I was just tying the laces on my skate."

"I was born during the day, but not yesterday," barked Aunt Zephyr. "Don't try your Little Miss Innocent routine on me. If there's one thing I know, it's an eaves-dropper!"

"So what if I did overhear?" Madison countered. "What are you going to do about it?"

"For one, I might have a talk with your mother, young miss! I might tell her that not only are you an eavesdropper, but you are also disrespectful to your elders."

"Go ahead," Madison dared her. "I'm already going to tell on Aleca. And when I do, I'll also tell everything I just heard!"

"You didn't hear anything," I proclaimed. I guess I felt sort of bold, now that I knew Madison wasn't a Wonder and didn't know my big secret. But at the same time, I was also going back through what Aunt Zephyr and I had just said. Madison didn't really know anything, did she?

"Oh, yes I did!" Madison raged. "I heard

your aunt say that you're not a normal ten-year-old girl! I *knew* something was weird about you! And now I have proof!"

"She's got us there, Aleca," Aunt Zephyr stated.

"Huh?" I was shocked. It wasn't like Aunt Zephyr to give up so fast. I would have thought Madison would be no match for her.

"She knows your secret," Aunt Zephyr acknowledged.

Why would she say such a thing? Had we not just performed scientific tickling to prove that Madison *didn't* know my secret?

"Aha! I was right!" bragged Madison. "See? I knew it! You have a secret! And now I know what it is! You're not normal!"

"You're absolutely right," Aunt Zephyr conceded. "Aleca is far from normal."

Madison crossed her arms and grinned in triumph.

"Normal girls are average," Aunt Zephyr continued. "Alike. The same. Run of the mill, you might say. Like you, for example. And Aleca, though she might look like an average girl, is far from ordinary. Instead, she is *extraordinarily* kind and selfless. That's why she skated onto the rink floor in just the nick of time to break my fall. What average girl would have such complete disregard for her own safety? No, Aleca is not your normal, everyday girl. Not at all."

Madison's triumphant grin slowly wilted into a frown.

"So when you're tattling on Aleca about whatever it is, be sure to tell your mother—and anyone else you'd like—all about how

98

extraordinary my Aleca is," crowed Aunt Zephyr.

"Yeah," Madison decided, "I'll get right on that." Just then Jordan skated over. "Thank goodness you're back, Jordan. I'm dying of boredom." The two linked arms and skated away.

"That was a close one," Aunt Zephyr declared. She closed the party room door. "Now, back to our discussion."

# ✳ 10 ✳

## The Most Disappointing
## Tattling in the History of Ever

When everyone gathered in the party room
a few minutes later to cut my birthday cake,
Madison tapped my mom on the shoulder.
"May I talk to you a minute, Mrs. Zamm?"
she asked.

"I'm a little busy right now, Madison," my
mom replied. "Can we wait until after I light
the candles and serve Aleca's cake?"

"It will only take a minute," Madison said.
"And it's important. It's about Aleca."

I followed them outside the party room. "This is private," Madison snapped.

My mom spoke up. "Madison, if you want to talk to me about Aleca, I think she has a right to be here."

"Fine," Madison sighed. "I just wondered if Aleca told you that she got in trouble at school the other day. Mrs. Floberg had to get *the principal* involved."

"Oh," Mom replied. "Yes, Aleca mentioned that to me. Something about your writing her name on the board when she hadn't done anything wrong?"

Madison gulped. That was not the reaction she'd been going for. "Well," Madison began, "a bunch of really weird stuff happened right after that. I don't know exactly how, but I'm sure Aleca was behind it."

Mom patted Madison on the head like she was a golden retriever who'd just brought back a tennis ball. Then Mom said in a superfake voice, "What a vivid imagination you have, Madison."

"B-but—" Madison sputtered.

"Aleca told me all about what happened at school. And frankly, I think you should be very glad that I chose not to discuss it with *your* mother."

Madison didn't know how to recover. "I . . . just thought . . . you should know. I was only trying to help."

Mom patted her head again and said in her phony voice, "If I need your help, I'll let you know. Are we finished here?"

"Yes," Madison replied.

"Wonderful," Mom said. "Then why don't

we go back inside and enjoy some birthday cake?" It was kind of the most awesome burn ever, because there is nothing more embarrassing than being totally owned and then offered cake. It's like the person who put you in your place is so cool that they didn't even notice that they just destroyed you.

Mom went back inside the party room, leaving Madison and me alone.

"Wow, Madison," I said. "That was probably the worst tattling anyone has ever done. Thanks for making this my best birthday ever!"

# ❋ 11 ❋

## My New Ally (Which Is What Spies Call People on Their Side, and Being a Spy Is Kind of Exciting)

When I got home that night, I was tired but couldn't make my brain shut down. The party had been fun, even in spite of Madison and Jordan, but after I'd found out about Ford, it had been hard to focus on having a good time.

Aunt Zephyr and I had decided that we would treat Ford as an ally. Mainly because we didn't know what else to do with him.

He already knew about my ability anyway, so there wasn't much risk in sharing information with him. We hoped that finding out more about him and what he knew might help us better understand Wonders in general. Ford was supersmart, after all, and he was the first and only Wonder that Aunt Zephyr had ever met who wasn't part of our family.

So my next job was to seek out Ford at school and try to talk to him in private. I wasn't sure how to do that, since he was only in third grade, and third graders and fourth graders were never on the playground or in the lunchroom together. But Aunt Zephyr said she was confident I'd find a way. Of course, even if I did find an opportunity to talk to him, that was no guarantee that

I could make any sense of what he said. He might just start talking about math and science again. But I had to try.

Maria was sound asleep in my other twin bed, and I could hear Aunt Zephyr snoring away in Dylan's room when a solution finally popped into my head.

I got out of bed and tiptoed to my desk. For my birthday Maria had given me some pretty notecards with colorful zigzags all over them and a big *A* in the center. I took one out of the package and wrote a note to Ford:

> We need to talk.
> Meet me at the playground swings
> before school on Tuesday.
> Tell no one.
> —A

I supposed the *A* at the end might have been overkill, since there was already an *A* on the card, but how else was I supposed to sign it?

I'd slip into Ford's classroom Monday morning, find his desk, and leave the note there for him to find. Then he would meet me Tuesday before school, and I'd get some answers.

I turned off the light, got back into bed, and closed my eyes. Aunt Zephyr's snores from the next room kept a regular rhythm, and I told myself there was nothing else to do but sleep.

Tuesday would be here before I knew it.

# Acknowledgments

Thanks again to my editor, Amy Cloud, for all your hard work on this series and for thinking I am funny. I think you are brilliant, so maybe that makes us even. Thanks to the rest of the team at Aladdin/Simon & Schuster for believing in Aleca and bringing her to life.

Thanks to my incredible agent and friend Abigail Samoun. What can I say? You are just the best.

Thank you to my bilingual friends Justin Brasfield, Dr. Krista Chambless, and Dr. Shirin Posner for filling in the gaps between online translations and my last foreign language class in college, which was . . . ahem . . . a while ago. Y'all are totally *bueno* and stuff.

Thanks to my family and friends for their continued support. Especially to my children and my nieces and nephews for their enthusiasm, critiques, and all those answers to my many, many questions. I love you all so much. And don't worry—I won't tell anyone that you are all Wonders. It will be our secret.

Finally, I would be remiss if I failed to thank my incredible husband, even though he prefers to stay in the background. Dwight, this would be infinitely less fun without you. I love you so.

**Don't miss the next book:**
*Aleca Zamm Fools Them All*

# Nancy Drew
## * CLUE BOOK *

Test your detective skills with Nancy and her best friends, Bess and George!

**NancyDrew.com**

# FUR AND FUN FLY AT THE ANIMAL INN— A SPA AND HOTEL FOR PETS!

A Furry Fiasco

Treasure Hunt

The Bow-wow Bus

Looking for another great book?
Find it
**IN THE MIDDLE**.

Fun, fantastic books for kids
in the in-be**TWEEN** age.

IntheMiddleBooks.com

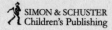